In Grandma's Day

Acknowledgments

Executive Editor: Diane Sharpe

Supervising Editor: Stephanie Muller

Design Manager: Sharon Golden

Page Design: Simon Balley Design Associates

Photography: Archiv fur Kunst und Geschichte: page 19 (color picture); Hulton Deutsch Collection: cover (middle), pages 9 (main picture), 15, 20, 22-23, 24-25, 26, 27; National Motor Museum/N. Wright: cover (top), page 13; Popperfoto: pages 11, 19, 26-27; Topham: page 7; V & A Picture Library: pages 9 (inset pictures), 17 (both).

Library of Congress Cataloging-in-Publication Data

Humphrey, Paul, 1952-

    In Grandma's day/Paul Humphrey; illustrated by Katy Sleight.

       p.   cm. — (Read all about it)

    Includes index.

    Summary: While visiting their grandma, two children learn about what life was like when she was young.

    ISBN 0-8114-5730-3 Hardcover

    ISBN 0-8114-3717-5 Softcover

    [1. Grandmothers — Fiction.] I. Sleight, Katy, ill. II. Title. III. Series: Read all about it (Austin, Tex.) Social studies. Level A.

PZ7.H8973In 1995

[E]—dc20

94-27317

CIP

AC

1 2 3 4 5 6 7 8 9 0 PO 00 99 98 97 96 95 94

STECK-VAUGHN
READ ALL ABOUT IT

In Grandma's Day

Paul Humphrey

Illustrated by

Katy Sleight

STECK-VAUGHN
COMPANY
ELEMENTARY • SECONDARY • ADULT • LIBRARY

4

Are you very old, Grandma?

6

Yes, but I was young once.

7

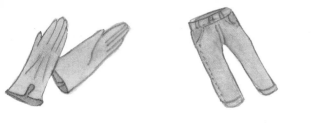

When I was young, people wore clothes like this.

When I was young, the streets looked like this.

What were cars like when you were young, Grandma?

When I was young, cars looked
like this.

When I was young, trains looked
like this.

What were toys like when you were young, Grandma?

When I was young, toys were like this.

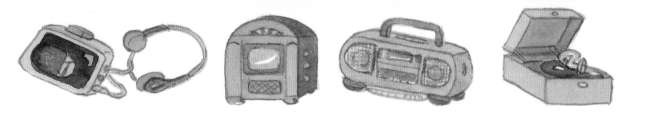

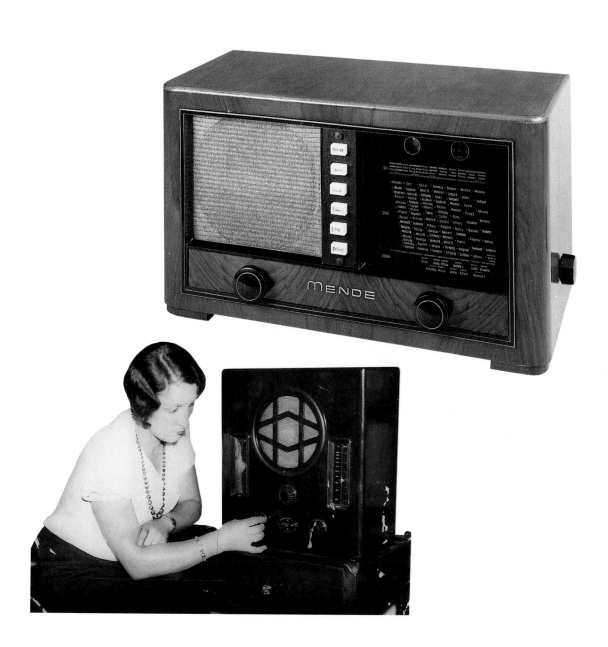

When I was young, I listened to the radio.

When I was young, I went dancing.

21

When I was young, people rode bicycles.

Really, Grandma?

23

When I was young, I went to the beach.

24

You had fun when you were young, Grandma.

Yes, I did.

What else happened when you were young, Grandma?

My grandma kissed me good night just like this.

29

Some of the things on this
page belong to Grandma's time.
Some belong to today. Which
ones are which?